To Ken and David

Father's Day Text copyright © 2005 by Anne Rockwell Illustrations copyright © 2005 by Lizzy Rockwell
Manufactured in China by South China Printing Company Ltd. All rights reserved.
www.harperchildrens.com   Library of Congress Cataloging-in-Publication Data   Rockwell, Anne F.
Father's Day / story by Anne Rockwell ; pictures by Lizzy Rockwell.— 1st ed.   p. cm. Summary: For
Father's Day, the students in Mrs. Madoff's class write and illustrate books about their dads. ISBN 0-06-
051377-2 — ISBN 0-06-051378-0 (lib. bdg.) [1. Fathers—Fiction. 2. Father's Day—Fiction. 3. Schools—
Fiction.] I. Rockwell, Lizzy, ill. II. Title. PZ7.R5943Fat 2005 2004006243 [E]—dc22 CIP AC
Typography by Elynn Cohen 1 2 3 4 5 6 7 8 9 10 ❖ First Edition

Father's Day

by Anne Rockwell   pictures by Lizzy Rockwell

HarperCollinsPublishers

Today we are making books about our dads.
I'm writing about how my dad is so strong,
he can still carry me.

I'm as tall as the sky
when I'm up on his shoulders.

"Papa sings his favorite song to me
if Maman has to work at night," Eveline said.
"It's the one his maman and papa sang to him."
She hummed the tune,
and we stopped writing to listen.
Mrs. Madoff reminded us,
"Remember—we need
quiet when we write."
So Eveline stopped humming,
and we went back to work.

After a while Evan raised his hand.
"How do you spell 'skillet'?"
he asked Mrs. Madoff.
She said, "S-K-I-L-L-E-T."
He erased something he'd written
and wrote it again.
I was sure he was writing about the camping trip
he and his dad went on—
just the two of them.
Evan told me that they slept in a tent
and cooked bacon and eggs in a skillet.

Jessica chewed on the end of her pencil.

"I don't know who to write about," she whispered.

"I have two fathers—my dad, who lives in Texas, and Lou, who lives here with me and Mom."

"Write about both of them," I said.

"Hey! Why didn't I think of that?" she said.

When it was time to read what we'd written,
Charlie went first.
"My father is a terrific person.
He has lots of friends, and I know why.
He never gets mad or loses his patience.
He says he can't, because when you're the
pilot of a big jet plane,
you always have to keep your cool."

Jessica read next.
"I have two fathers and love them both.
My dad, Bradley, lives in Texas
and knows all about horses.
My stepfather, Lou, has never even been
on a horse.
He always plays gigglebugs with me
after work, even if he's tired."

Sarah read, "My father is great at everything—
yes—everything in the world.
He's such a great cook, he should be a chef on TV.
You should taste his chocolate marshmallow minty fudge!
It's delicious!"

Pablo held his paper close to his face.
"I feel so proud when Papi and I play soccer.
Papi shows me how to kick and dribble.
Every time I practice with him, I get better.
Papi plays on a team in town with his friends.
He says that one day
I'll be a better player than him!"

Kate said, "I wrote a poem for my dad.
Is that okay?"
"Of course," said Mrs. Madoff.
Kate read her poem, which went—
"Daddy taught me to dive
and to find a beehive.
When I caught three shiny fish,
we put them in a yellow dish."

"For a long time I drew pictures of me
in a bright pink room," Michiko said.
"I told my father how much I wanted
a bright pink room.
One day we went to the hardware store
and now my dream has come true!
My father and I painted my room Summer Rose
because that's the color I picked."

"My dad reads all the time," Nicholas read.
"We like reading the same kind of books."

After lunch we took our stories
to the publishing center.
Michiko's mother was helping there that day.
She printed copies for all the dads.

On the Friday in June before Father's Day,
we came to school with our dads.
We gave them our books.

All of a sudden a man in a cowboy hat
got out of a pickup truck and ran to Jessica.
"Dad! I didn't know you were coming!" she said
as they hugged each other.
"I wanted to surprise you," he said.
Jessica had two dads at the Father's Day picnic.

We had cupcakes and brownies.
Sarah said the brownies were almost as good
as the ones her dad makes.
My dad read his book again and again.
Each time he read it, he gave me a hug.